Table of Contents

Detention for Timothy Michael McCall 5

Timothy Meets the Bad Guys 9

Captain Hook's Tale 13

The Giant's Tale 15

The Witch's Tale 17

The Evil Stepsisters' Tale 19

Goldilocks's Tale 21

The Wolf's Tale 23

Timothy's Turn 25

A Lesson Learned? 29

About Us 32

Detention for Timothy Michael McCall

I am Timothy Michael McCall.
Please don't ever call me "Tim,"
or "Timmy" or "Mike" or "Micky."
My name has no synonym!

Earlier today in science class,
an incredible occurrence did befall.
I answered a question like I always do,
but the teacher ushered me out to the hall.

She said, "It's time to finally terminate
your inappropriate actions."
"But what did I do? I'm not noisy,
or sleepy, nor do I cause silly distractions!"

"Well, Mr. Timothy Michael McCall,
you know better than asking me that.
When you knowingly break the rules,
it's off to *special* detention. Now scat!"

She handed me a fold-up map
and pointed down the hall.
"Come back when you've learned your lesson,
Mr. Timothy Michael McCall!"

Being the good kid I've always been,
I followed my teacher's command,
and I tried my best to follow the map,
but it was so easy to misunderstand!

I finally came to some stairs
that I had never noticed before.
I descended into darkness quite carefully
and came to an ancient door.

I pushed the big door open—
of course it groaned and creaked.
The map said go to the door on the left.
My curiosity piqued.

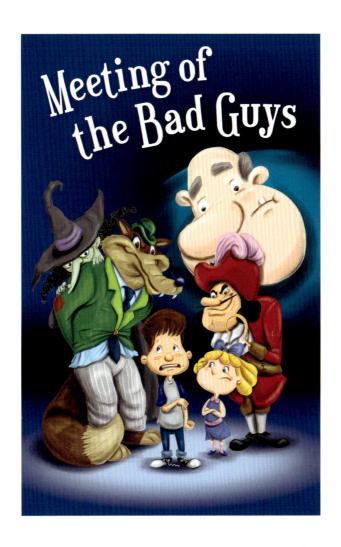

Meeting of
the Bad Guys

By Joe Rhatigan
Illustrated by Brian Martin

Publishing Credits

Rachelle Cracchiolo, M.S.Ed., *Publisher*
Conni Medina, M.A.Ed., *Editor in Chief*
Nika Fabienke, Ed.D., *Content Director*
Véronique Bos, *Creative Director*
Shaun N. Bernadou, *Art Director*
Susan Daddis, M.A.Ed., *Editor*
John Leach, *Assistant Editor*
Jess Johnson, *Graphic Designer*

Image Credits

Illustrated by Brian Martin

Library of Congress Cataloging-in-Publication Data

Names: Rhatigan, Joe, author. | Martin, Brian (Brian Michael), 1978-
  illustrator.
Title: Meeting of the bad guys / by Joe Rhatigan ; illustrated by Brian
  Martin.
Description: Huntington Beach, CA : Teacher Created Materials, [2020] |
  Includes book club questions. | Audience: Age 12. | Audience: Grades
  4-6.
Identifiers: LCCN 2019026029 (print) | LCCN 2019026030 (ebook) | ISBN
  9781644913338 (paperback) | ISBN 9781644914236 (ebook)
Subjects: LCSH: Readers (Elementary) | Characters and characteristics in
  literature--Juvenile fiction. | Human behavior--Juvenile fiction.
Classification: LCC PE1119 .R4635 2020 (print) | LCC PE1119 (ebook) | DDC
  428.6/2--dc23
LC record available at https://lccn.loc.gov/2019026029
LC ebook record available at https://lccn.loc.gov/2019026030

5301 Oceanus Drive
Huntington Beach, CA 92649-1030
www.tcmpub.com

ISBN 978-1-6449-1333-8

Printed by 51250
PO 10851 / Printed in USA

As I approached, I heard the words
villain, scoundrel, and *lout.*
I walked in angrily and asked,
"Wait! Who are you talking about?"

The question died on my tongue
as I saw who was inside the room.
I thought: *There's been a horrible mistake,
and I'm about to meet my doom!*

Because inside the room was a chalkboard
and desks where students could sit.
But those desks weren't filled with students!
Inside was a slew of fairy-tale miscreants!

A pirate, a witch, the Big Bad Wolf,
a giant whose head scraped the ceiling.
Two angry-looking sisters and Goldilocks!
This class of evil dudes had me reeling.

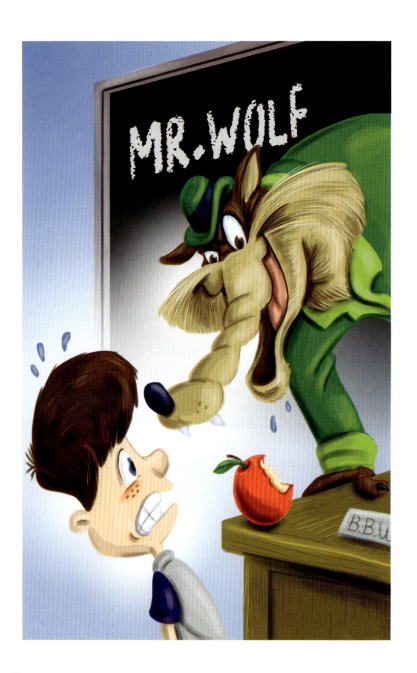

Timothy Meets the Bad Guys

At the head of the class stood the Big Bad Wolf,
whose grin looked like a scowl.
"I am about to begin my session.
Sit and be quiet," he said with a growl.

"Mr. Wolf," I interjected.
"What are you talking about?
The idea that I belong in here with you,
is a notion I rather doubt."

I tried to get the wolf's attention
and refuse his invitation,
but Wolf said, "Stop interrupting!"
So I sat with my growing frustration.

"We're all here to learn something important,
like how to take the blame
for all the poor decisions we made,
so we can restore all our good names."

"That's well and fine," I said,
"and here is definitely where you guys belong.
But you can't say I'm a fit here,
as I don't know what I've done wrong!"

"I'm beginning to get an idea
of why you've ended up down here.
But if we follow the process,
I believe everything will become clear.

"Because everyone here has a story.
Sit back to listen and learn,
and after waiting patiently,
you will have a turn…

"…to tell us all your story
so we can see what your detention's about—
what caused your teacher such misery
that she had to throw you out.

10

"But first, an introduction:
Yes, I'm that sneaky, sharp-toothed barbarian,
but now I do yoga and meditate,
and I recently became a vegetarian.

"I took a course, passed the test,
and have a certificate of completion,
which states I can teach each of you here
how to avoid future detention.

"One by one I'll listen,
and with my expertise,
I'll give you advice that is helpful
so you can become as reformed as me.

"Who wants to get us started?" he asked.
And the pirate raised a hook.
I recognized him right away
from my Peter Pan picture book.

Captain Hook's Tale

"I'm Captain Hook, as you can tell,
and I would like to go first.
I know that I've behaved poorly,
but that Peter Pan is the worst.

"It's all his fault I lost everything:
my crew, my gold, my boat.
He lopped off my hand and teased me
and loved to brag and gloat.

"I was trying to be a good pirate,
and it really is a crime
that, no matter how cruel I had to be,
Peter started it every time."

"Now, now," said the Big Bad Wolf,
"you're not faultless in this story.
You kidnapped Pan's friends and threatened them
with tortures grim and gory.

"Your first step is to acknowledge
the blame that's yours alone."
"But I want to tell my side," said Hook.
Wolf answered, "That's not how you atone."

Wolf and Captain Hook argued
for seventeen minutes at least,
until we heard a pounding noise
from the gigantic, fantastical beast.

The Giant's Tale

"It's my turn now," said the Giant,
and you don't need an advanced degree
to know that when someone that big wants his
turn,
that it's best to nod and agree.

"They call me a villain and scoundrel,
or quite a miserable louse,
but anyone who knows me," said the Giant,
"knows that I wouldn't harm a mouse.

"My home was invaded by a thieving boy
who wanted my gold egg-laying goose.
He stole my cash, then tried to kill me.
Why should I have to put up with such abuse?"

The Big Bad Wolf shook his head sadly,
"That's not the way to repent.
You must be held accountable
One hundred and fifty percent!

"Maybe if you didn't overreact
and were more generous with your gold,
Jack wouldn't have been so desperate
to steal from your household."

The Giant started to chant
his "fee-fi-fo" and "fum,"
and I think he would have eaten us
if I hadn't given him all my gum.

The Witch's Tale

"My story demands to be heard next!" said the
Witch.
"That Hansel and Gretel, I had to grab 'em.
They ignored my 'No Trespassing' sign
and were eating up my cabin."

Wolf stood there shaking his head,
"You know that argument isn't a winner.
They were starving and nibbling on your roof.
That's no reason to prepare them as dinner."

"I thought that they were chickens!
You know my eyesight's so poor.
Such big fowl, I reckoned,
I'd have supper, leftovers, and more."

"By now you will remember," said Wolf,
"the reason for this class is
to recognize excuses and lies,
because I know that you have glasses."

"Gretel fell into the oven," the Witch replied.
"Hansel just wandered into that cage.
None of this was my fault at all!"
the Witch said, in a rage.

"In order to seek forgiveness," Wolf replied,
"you have to see your truth:
you like eating up children,
which is evil and uncouth."

The Evil Stepsisters' Tale

"Our turn, our turn," said the sisters,
whose mom married Cinderella's dad.
"That silly girl was a show-off,
and that really made us mad.

"We didn't have any magic
or a godmother to make us a dress.
If Cinderella could do things for herself,
we wouldn't be in this mess.

"Her father really spoiled her,
so we made her mow the lawn,
darn our dresses, sleep in the fireplace,
and with her toothbrush, clean the john."

"You can try to blame the victim," said Wolf.
"We've all tried it once or twice before.
But jealousy leads to behaviors
that princes tend to deplore.

"You won't become better people
until you accept more fully
the fact that you lost that prince
because you were both such bullies.

"If you were less bitter and spiteful,
Cinderella may have shared that fairy.
But, instead, you drove her crazy,
and she's the one the prince did marry."

Goldilocks's Tale

Goldilocks's hair bounced as she talked,
"My story is unique as you will see,
because it wasn't me in the bears' house at all.
It was a case of mistaken identity."

Wolf cut in, "There's video evidence,
and the cops put you in jail.
Little Red Riding Hood got you out,
and then you skipped out on the bail."

"Riding Hood, she's the one
who broke the little bear's chair.
And I'm much too young and pretty
to eat porridge fit for a bear."

"That's a wonderful fib," said Wolf,
"that no one here will buy,
because Little Red Riding Hood
has an ironclad alibi.

"Little Red was with me," said Wolf,
"at the time the crime took place.
I had just swallowed her grandma,
much to my own disgrace!"

Every villain and rogue in the room
let out an audible gasp.
We moved our chairs back away from Wolf
to avoid his hungry grasp.

The Wolf's Tale

"Let me explain," Wolf replied.
"Don't worry, I spit her right out.
Grandma was fine and dandy
by the time we left her house.

"Calling someone 'bad' is…pretty bad, you know,
well, 'Bad' is actually my middle name!
I try so hard to fight who I am,
but some days there's no escaping the shame.

"I know my name is but an excuse
for my poor behavior.
Taking responsibility
Has surely been my savior.

"Yes, I blew down two piggies' homes,
but I said that I had the flu
and it was only a giant sneeze.
It was a lie everyone saw through.

"But then I stopped to think about
my reasons for being there.
I have to admit I was hungry,
and the smell of bacon was in the air.

"So while 'bad' is right there in my name,
I try to resist my base impulses,
but some days when I see pigs or grandmothers,
my actions are still repulsive."

Timothy's Turn

I couldn't wait any longer and said,
"Even though I don't belong with the likes of you,
I have my own observations,
such as: so much of what Wolf says is untrue!

"First of all, the villain of a story
is known as the antagonist.
It's his or her job to do wicked things,
to make it hard for the good guys to exist.

"Of course, you fail because you must,
that's how a fairy tale works,
but you should at least get to have fun acting badly!
I think you should sit back and enjoy those perks!

"Because a kid like me never gets away
with anything wrong at all.
Anytime I move a muscle, it's detention for
Timothy Michael McCall.

"If I was the bad guy in a story,
I'd certainly enjoy the ride
and hope at least a few kids reading
would understand my side.

"I think we need to take a moment
to acknowledge the good things you do.
For instance, Captain Hook, old pal,
you keep a neat ship for your mutinous crew.

"And, Giant, you may be monstrous
with nothing but murder in your heart.
But you were protecting your house from a thief.
You're simply too easy to outsmart.

"Witch, while eating children may be a bit much,
those kids were pests, indeed.
They learned a valuable lesson from you:
Next time, they'll stop and read!

"Stepsisters, sure you were jealous,
but it's not fair to use magic to win.
I bet that prince is a boring old brat
with no brains behind that silly grin.

"Wolf, it isn't your middle name
that tells you who you are.
It's your last one: Wolf! You are literally a wolf!
Of course you want to eat pigs and grandmas!"

"What about me?" asked Goldilocks.
"Well your behavior had me shocked.
But even though you're a convicted felon,
those bears *did* leave their door unlocked."

The nasties cheered me mightily,
and threw me in the air.
Wolf looked on disapprovingly,
but I didn't even care.

A Lesson Learned?

"I think I now have a notion," said Wolf,
"of why from class you were banned.
You seem to have all the answers,
but do you ever raise your hand?"

I bragged, "Well, without raising my hand even
once,
I called out thirty-two times in a row.
And while I should vow to do better,
I have all the right answers, you know.

"And I think that what I've learned today
from all of you fairy-tale guys,
is that we are who we are and cannot change,
so there's no reason to compromise."

The Big Bad Wolf rubbed his chinny chin chin,
"Today's results are less than desired.
If you haven't learned to change your behavior,
my session today has backfired.

"Maybe it is our job to be scoundrels
in fairy tales and lore,
but you are not in a story,
and that makes you nothing more than a bore.

"I pronounce you the baddest guy," said Wolf.
"As you won't change your ways, I assume.
Please know I feel awful for any teacher
who has Timothy Michael McCall in her room."

About Us

The Author

Joe Rhatigan is an author and book editor who occasionally forgets to raise his hand but always apologizes afterward. Joe has written such books as *Everyone Toots*, *I Love a Book*, and dozens more. He lives in Asheville, North Carolina, with a dog named Rooster and the rest of his family.

The Illustrator

Brian Martin is an author and illustrator from Richmond, Virginia. As an illustrator, he loves to tell stories with his bright and whimsical art and has illustrated over 30 children's books. He is always looking for opportunities to bring stories to life for both children and parents to enjoy. When he isn't busy writing or making art, he enjoys playing with his four amazing kids.